OPEN AND SHUT CASES

40 MORE MINI-MYSTERIES
FOR YOU TO SOLVE

OPEN AND SHUT CASES

40 More Mini-Mysteries for You to Solve

JÜRG OBRIST

MILLBROOK PRESS

MINNEAPOLIS

Published in the United States of America in 2006 by
Millbrook Press

Originally published in Germany by dtv junior
www.dtvjunior.de

Copyright © 1999 by Deutscher Taschenbuch Verlag GmbH & Co.
KG Munich
Translation copyright © 2006 by Jürg Obrist

Millbrook Press
A division of Lerner Publishing Group
241 First Avenue North
Minneapolis, Minnesota 55401 U.S.A.

Website address: www.lernerbooks.com

Library of Congress Cataloging-in-Publication Data

Obrist, Jürg.
    [Klarer Fall?! English.]
    Open and shut cases: 40 more mini-mysteries for you to solve /
by Jürg Obrist.
        p.   cm.
    Summary: The reader can use visual clues and deductive
reasoning to help Daisy and Ridley solve forty puzzling mysteries.
    Includes solutions
        ISBN–13: 978–0–7613–2740–0 (lib. bdg.)
        ISBN–10: 0–7613–2740–1 (lib. bdg.)
    [1. Detectives – Fiction. 2. Mystery and detective stories.]
    I. Title.
    PZ7.O14Op 2006
    [Fic]–dc22   2003014140

Manufactured in the United States of America
1 2 3 4 5 6 – BP – 11 10 09 08 07 06

CONTENTS

ON THE JOB WITH DAISY AND RIDLEY

"All set!" Ridley Long hollers, and puts on his tattered coat. Daisy Pepper has already slipped out the door. The two detectives are on their way to solve a new mystery. They are good at their jobs, but they can always use a little help—and we can learn a few things from them as well. So let's go along with them on their next few cases.

Just be careful! Crooks can be very sneaky and they don't always tell the truth. Read the text carefully and examine the pictures closely, because they contain important clues. They'll help you to work with Ridley and Daisy to solve the mysteries.

If you're all set, then let's go!

THE MYSTERIOUS MOUSTACHE

When Major Pensley arrived in his office early this morning, he discovered the most embarrassing thing. The portrait of himself, which the artist had delivered just last week, had a big ugly moustache drawn on top of it!

"This must have happened last night," Pensley shouts. He immediately calls for Daisy Pepper's help.

When she sees the nasty moustache on Pensley's portrait, Daisy murmurs, "Gee, he wasn't kidding!" and she dashes out the door. She is going to pay a visit to Nero Schlotzing, a well-known opponent of the major. Just yesterday evening he had been heard bragging that he would show Pensley what he thinks of his using the people's tax money to have his own personal portrait painted.

At 8 A.M. sharp Daisy rings Schlotzing's doorbell. She gets right down to business, and accuses him of drawing that moustache on Pensley's portrait. Naturally, Schlotzing is insulted by the accusation: "Why, I slept like a baby in my bed last night, and have just now gotten up. As a matter of fact, I haven't set foot out the door for the last twelve hours." Daisy knows better. She has already discovered proof that Schlotzing is lying.

What is the proof that Daisy found?

THE NARROW ESCAPE

At the Morningside bus station, the bus to Kingslaw City is ready for boarding. A ten-hour journey lies ahead. Ridley, disguised as a tourist, joins the travelers. In fact, he is after a smuggler of fake caviar who is supposed to be on the bus. Ridley has never seen the smuggler. But he has been informed that the scoundrel is taking one of his "business trips." And Ridley wants to catch him on the job.

Soon all the passengers' baggage is stowed away in the luggage compartment of the bus. But wait a minute! Ridley is astounded to see only eighteen pieces of luggage! Just a minute ago he had counted nineteen. The smuggler must have recognized Ridley, grabbed his luggage, and quickly disappeared!

Which person is the smuggler?

WANTED

Daisy and Ridley are on the tracks of the notorious Romeo, Dino Sweely. He has tricked many rich women into trusting him and believing his proposals of marriage. Daisy and Ridley know that Dino often goes to spas and health resorts in search of his future "wives."

But at Youngwater's Resort, the swindler makes a crucial mistake. Unwittingly, he tries his luck on Ridley's aunt, Antonia Dole. Antonia immediately telephones her nephew and tells him about the impostor.

She is able to give Ridley an exact description:

Black hair, black moustache, glasses, white shirt, black jacket, white pants. Seen around the Hotel Winterlake.

Ridley and Daisy hurry to the hotel. They are in luck. The detectives discover Dino among the many guests. Where is Dino?

IS HOBBARD MANSION STALKY'S HIDEOUT?

Stalky fled prison a few days ago. The police suspect that he is hiding in the old, abandoned Hobbard mansion. But they don't have enough people to observe the house twenty-four hours a day. So they call Ridley and Daisy onto the job.

They hide in an apartment opposite the mansion.

Ridley is first on the night watch. But–typical!–he falls asleep and wakes up just when Daisy arrives for her turn. How embarrassing! But Daisy isn't mad, for she sees immediately that Stalky spent the night in Hobbard mansion.

What changed between yesterday and today?

THE TOP-SECRET MARS VEHICLE

Professor Schulz talks excitedly to Daisy: "While I was in the coffee shop around the corner, someone must have gone through my desk. There are some top-secret plans for my new Mars vehicle. I've been working on it for years now, and I'm about to make a breakthrough." The Professor suspects that one of his three assistants wants to give important information about the Mars vehicle to Schulz's competitors.

"If that's the case, we will find out who has been sneaking around!" replies Daisy. She wants to question each one of Schulz's assistants. Of course they are astonished by the professor's suspicions. This is what they have to say:

Mike Schletz: "I was in the lab the whole morning. I didn't even know about the professor's secret plans."

Will Poke: "I was at my desk all morning long. I couldn't have read the secret plans since I accidentally left my reading glasses at home."

Dirk Klein: "I arrived just a few minutes ago, and only had time to make myself a cup of coffee. I didn't look at the documents on the professor's desk."

It is clear to Daisy which one of the three is lying.

Who is it, and what is Daisy's proof?

THE ODD SAFE

Rod Steeler is very confused. Daisy and Ridley look at the safe that stands in the middle of his junkyard. He explains what happened: "This morning a shabby-looking fellow drove up in a truck and quietly unloaded this rusty safe in my yard. He told me that the police would be very interested in its contents. He also hinted that there would be important information about the wicked Moscito Gang and its whereabouts, claiming to be a former member of the gang himself. Then he jumped into his truck and took off."

When Daisy and Ridley examine the safe they notice a little note stuck on the door. On it is written:

"ONLY BUSY BEES WITH A CALCULATOR
WILL OPEN ME!"

"I have a calculator," Daisy laughs. "I might as well try to crack the number lock's combination. I'll bet it's a four-digit number we have to look for," she guesses.

They try many number combinations. At 5, 3, 3, they hear a click. "Not bad, just one more." Daisy's confidence grows. She enters the numbers into her calculator and tries all kinds of combinations.

Ridley only watches her. But all of a sudden he jumps up and shouts: "That's it. Bees, of course. I have got the fourth number!"

What does Ridley see, and what's the four-digit number?

WHO IS ZORO IN REAL LIFE?

Finally Daisy has the chance to track down Zoro, the boss of the Terrible 10 Gang. A secret paper has accidentally fallen into her hands. It's a strange entrance test for people who want to join the gang.

The test consists of several strange mathematical problems. The correct answers reveal Zoro's private telephone number. And the only way to get in touch with the mighty boss is by telephone. "Once I have his number I'll be able to find his real name and address in the telephone book," Daisy says triumphantly.

Math was never Daisy's strong point . . . but with a lot of sweat and persistence, she finally cracks the code. "That's it for you, Mister," she cheers.

What's Zoro's real name, address, and telephone number?

PRIVATE   MABLOW - MUZ

Wane------546-8794   Melow Burt
gham P. 3 Essex   lawyer-------- 456-9825
st 33-------- 568-8702   Meluny plumbing
n Louiza   Stanford Rd---443-7223
a Bosly --- 678-8790   Memmling Sid 45 Doosly Rd
on Carl   Rdg-----------443-8965
ring Pl.--- 567-3349   Memo Family
Phil 8 Crmen Rd   East drive----- 560-3356
----------675-4509   Mempot & Sondler
g Inc.   Trade---------- 424-8027
Pw-------785-0983   Mendoz Juan
& W   33 Sern Rd---- 543-7965
ing Rd--- 567-3290   Menning Stamps
Peter   4 Zucker lane---443-7239
g Lane- 443-8762   Mennwood Lucy
acy   37 Potter sq---- 576-7925
---------- 478-7765   Mibbson Mel
                           Willmington--- 443-7864
state----560-2349   Mifter Mary Racing
Joe J   office--------- 345-4398
Plaza--548-8332   home--------- 433-2579
nda insurance   Migger Jack
ch----443-7752   Stubbly Av--- 549-5639
Carl   Miklander Inc. Trading
& So-- 549-8760   4 Stew Av--- 445-8407
v   Mikonnen Jon
---- 443-5982   plumbing------- 539-8873
n   Miller Fred
ply-- 443-7628   12 Main Street-443-7732
wels   Miller Automotive Svc Inc
----487-2727   International --- 380-7766
---- 465-7690   Milson Caren
                           New Port

Mitlow Tony
  2 Mc Dougal--- 443-7689
Mitzler Sonja
  haircutter----- 443-7867
Mobsman Frank
  used furniture - 377-8324
Mobster Inc.
Hardware--443-7203
Modler Paul
  Carpenting---- 487-9907
Mofy Mark & Jill
  7 Kensington--- 443-8765
Moghan John
  attorney at law- 539-8868
Moorksman family
  5 Zepfler Rd--- 443-7965
Mossing & Zepf
Accounting
  44 Fed. Plaza-- 443-5590
Mozzing Joshua
  Photographer-- 443-8734
Mubington Anna
  Walnut Av-----453-7926
Mudsonson
  Northern Food Inc.
  7 Wonton Rd--- 563-6532
Muddy Music
  31 Piano Blvd- 333-6678
Muglon Wilma

Mukmennen Jo
  Sport & Fun--- 327-4528
Muller Fred
  6 Woosley pw- 443-7635
Muller Debby
  28 Middle Rd-- 456-7952
Mummie Mory
  WO------------445-7627
Murbing Dan & Pat
  4 Dole Rd----- 459-5998
Murdane Ann
  P--------------421-7630
Murdoch Stuart News
  Nuthole--------443-7725
Murey Mobby
  W E----------- 358-7835
Murkey Floyd
  3 Ellwood Rd--443-7923
Murkmann Jane
  St. Martin----- 376-9776
Murrson Inc
  Seafood & Fish 457-7769
Murrting Dooly
  Fed Plaza----- 682-2243
Musby Elisabeth
  9 Lower Beach 453-6687
Mustacher Bert
  tobacco-------- 377-8221
Mustkin Ivan
  Horse supply

CIGARS IN DEEP SNOW

Ridley just wanted to buy a newspaper in Cole's Tobacco Shop this morning. But Mr. Cole is out of breath and very excited. "Yikes, someone just stole my most expensive box of Windlocks Cigars!" he shouts. "It must have happened between 8 o'clock and 8:15. That's when I was in the back of the shop to check a new shipment from the delivery truck."

Ridley tries to calm Cole down. Four people have been seen in front of the shop at the time in question. Here is what they have to say:

Liz Hutle claims she was in the shop for only a short time, to look at some tobacco pipes.

Donald Kraft says: "I didn't go inside the shop. I just stopped in front of it and looked in the window."

Kirk Mouser explains that he never entered the shop either. He simply walked by.

Agnes Fletcher assures Ridley she only went in to buy her daily supply of chewing gum. Cole wasn't around, so she left the money on the counter.

"One of these four is lying and most likely stole the fancy cigars!" Ridley tells Cole. "And I know exactly who it was!"

Do you know too?

Liz Hutle   Donald Kraft   Kirk Mouser   Agnes Fletcher

SWINESGATE PORCELAIN

Daisy has a passion for Swinesgate porcelain figures! She loves and collects these little treasures. And the only place where she can purchase them at a reasonable price is at the Arts and Crafts Fair held every Saturday on Lobster Place. Hank Trickler, an art dealer, sells them at his stand.

Daisy buys one of the cute rabbits for her collection. All of a sudden she has a strange feeling that the figure is not an original Swinesgate. It's very light, much lighter than porcelain! Could it actually be a cheap plastic copy? She is not the only one with this terrible suspicion. Other customers also realize that they have bought a fake. The tension in the crowd mounts. They surround Trickler and demand their money back. But Hank quickly grabs his money box and dashes across Lobster Place. "Follow him!" the angry crowd shouts. "He is running away with our money." They chase after him but are forced to stop to let a bus pass by.

Unfortunately, Trickler had enough of a lead to disappear before they could continue following him. At that moment, Mrs. Friskey shouts, "Look, he has run down to the Willbrook Canal!" She points to the stairs. "He fled through the abandoned tunnel."

Daisy takes a good look and shouts back to Mrs. Friskey, "That's not true! You must be in with Trickler, and are trying to get us off his track."

How does Daisy know that Mrs. Friskey is lying?

A GAME WITH SHIRT BUTTONS

It's late October–Halloween time in Chubby City! Even during these jolly celebrations, Ridley is on the job. Nick, the boss of the Octopus Tavern, has called him for help. When Ridley arrives, he finds Nick arguing with a man named Trenton Hook, who is dressed as a prisoner. Nick claims that Trenton has gambled with his slot machine using shirt buttons instead of coins, and that he completely emptied it of money. Trenton, on the other hand, assures Ridley that he wasn't in Nick's tavern at all. Suddenly he begins to sneeze, since he is wearing only an undershirt. "Let's go inside where it's warm. You'll catch a cold out here," Ridley says, and pulls him into the smoky tavern.

"He played here for more than an hour," Nick grumbles and points to the slot machine. "When I approached him to have a talk, he took off into the street!"

"That's baloney. I haven't set foot in this place tonight!" Trenton angrily replies. Ridley carefully takes a look around the busy place. Then he smiles and asks Trenton to admit the truth.

How does he know that Trenton is lying?

THE MAN WHO LOVES BEDS

Max Bedman loves to sleep in big luxurious beds! Not his own, of course. Max sneaks into department stores shortly before closing time. He hides in their bed departments. Once everybody has left, he cuddles up and sleeps in one of the fancy beds all night long. In the morning he secretly disappears. No one has ever seen him, they just find traces of him. His favorite bed is in Sleepyland, the famous bed and mattress store.

Alarmed by the odd nightly visitor, Sleepyland has installed video cameras. And indeed, one night they were able to tape Max happily snoring away. At last Daisy knows what the mysterious visitor looks like. She is hired to get Max back into his own bed!

This morning she is informed that Max has spent the night once again in Sleepyland. Daisy carefully watches the entrance as the store opens. But the sneaky sleeper doesn't leave. At this moment she notices some workers carrying mattresses from the delivery warehouse to a truck. "That's it," she smiles. "He could easily get out this way."

Is Daisy's hunch correct?

THE FAKE PACISSTO

The famous and valuable portrait *Gregoire* has been stolen from the Art Museum of Rubbleford. It's a painting by the artistic genius Paulo Pacissto. Now only the empty frame hangs on the wall. Ridley, who was called at once, suspects that Carlo Brushinsky, an amateur painter, could be involved in the theft. Carlo is known for copying valuable art. He then sells the copies for a lot of money to art lovers who think that they are buying the original paintings!

Ridley, on a hunch, decides to pay Carlo a visit. He can't believe his eyes when he surprises the painter, who is busily working in his studio. Carlo is painting ten identical-looking portraits like *Gregoire*. One of them must be the original and the others are copies. But Ridley, with his discerning eye, can quickly see that Carlo wasn't able to paint as exactly as he thinks! Only two of the paintings are truly identical: one of them a perfect copy and the other the original! The rest of the pictures all have slight differences. "Dr. Loop, the director of the art museum, will be quite pleased to have his original returned, as well as this exact copy," he laughs.

Which two of the portrait paintings will Ridley proudly bring to the art museum?

PHONY MAGIC

In the Nelsonville Amusement Park, the magician Abra Kabra performs his humble magic show. One of his tricks is to snatch watches and jewelry from the pockets of the astonished audience. Surely he must return the stolen goods at the end of the show. But here's his real trick—he returns only part of the valuables. In their excitement, the people don't get suspicious. Naturally he keeps the remaining loot for himself!

Of course afterward the people realize that their valuables are missing. But by then it is too late. They can't

prove that Abra Kabra is indeed the thief. So Daisy is called in to help. Even she can't pin the magician down. In desperation, she decides to follow him one evening after the show. He has to do something with the stuff he sneaks away with! Sure enough, Abra Kabra disappears into the Crow Bar around the corner. It's a well-known place for crooks and swindlers. Too bad Daisy has lost sight of the magician in the crowd.

Can you find the trickster in the bar?

THE PRECIOUS LOUIS PHILIPPE

Justin Stanislaw proudly shows Daisy and Ridley his small but fine collection of antique clocks and watches. All of a sudden he turns pale. "What's this!" he shouts, shocked. "My little Louis Philippe is gone!" He can't believe his eyes. "The Louis Philippe is my most valuable table clock. A work of art when it comes to clock-making, even though it usually is ten minutes slow." Stanislaw continues, "Just yesterday I showed the clock to Joe Waddler, a dealer in old clocks and watches. He was so excited, he wanted to buy it right away. But of course I wouldn't sell it for all the money in the world!"

Could Waddler have something to do with the disappearance of the Louis Philippe, Ridley wonders. Waddler is known as a person who always gets what he wants.

Daisy and Ridley promise Stanislaw to look into the matter. And soon enough they enter Waddler's store. They are surrounded by hundreds of ticking clocks and watches. "We are looking for a nice gift for my uncle," Daisy pretends. This way they can easily search for the Louis Philippe. After just a short time Daisy winks at Ridley. She has found what they are looking for!

Where is the little table clock, and why is Daisy sure that it is the Louis Philippe?

TRANSACTION AT THE SNACK BAR

Ridley is on the scent of the suspected spy, Will Wickley. Until now, Will had cleverly managed to hide his business and nobody could ever pin him to any wrongdoing. But Ridley has discovered that Will wants to hand over some top-secret information on a disc to another dubious swindler today! The transaction is scheduled to take place at 11:30 at the Rio Snack Bar. Ridley is ready and waiting at the Rio. He orders two hot dogs and a lemonade.

Ridley immediately spots Will. He is at a table, nibbling on a sausage. At 11:32 a suspicious-looking man arrives. As he passes Will's table, he turns toward him for a second, then slowly walks on.

Everything happened so quickly and Ridley only saw the men from the back. Yet he is sure that he saw the two men nod at each other. "Of course!" He suddenly smiles, as he realizes how the transaction took place!

What did Ridley see?

HECK DUNDEE AND THE CELLO

Things are in terrible turmoil at the train station—the valuable cello of the famous musician Edwin Stolcker has been stolen. Luckily, Ridley is already on the scene. A woman passing by claims to have seen a black-haired man running away, clutching a cello case. Her description fits the no-good bully Heck Dundee. Ridley knows all about Heck and has a feeling that he could be behind this terrible theft. It won't hurt to pay him a visit, Ridley decides. Heck lives with his brother, also a troublemaker, in a shed down at the river.

It's pitch black at the house. Only a small light is burning in the back. Ridley rings the doorbell. The door opens slowly and Heck peeks out. Ridley squints in the darkness. Grumbling, Heck lets Ridley in. "The light-bulb in the hallway is broken," he explains. "I'll get a lamp from the kitchen." Ridley follows Heck through the dark hallway. All of a sudden he bumps into something hard and stumbles.

Just then Heck comes out of the kitchen with a light. "Now what's this?" Ridley wonders. He had stumbled over a cello—Stolcker's cello! "How interesting," Ridley says, smirking.

Heck seems puzzled. "I've never seen this before. My brother must have left it there."

But you can't pull the wool over Ridley's eyes! He knows immediately that Heck himself must be the cello thief.

How does Ridley come to this conclusion?

THE MISSING DINOSAUR EGG

Daisy and her niece, Tracy, are visiting the Museum of Natural History. Tracy is a big fan of dinosaurs. When they arrive at the Dino Park, Tracy is puzzled. "Strange," she says. "As far as I know there were always three dinosaur eggs in here. Now I see only two of them!" Just then Dr. Pokley, the museum's director, Ned Windler, his assistant, and the cleaning lady, Betty, walk by. Tracy's remark makes them curious, and they come over immediately.

"You're right," Dr. Pokley says, shocked. "There should be three eggs. Yesterday evening all of them were still there. Somebody must have stolen one last night!"

Dr. Pokley asks his assistant, Windler, to bring the scientific data about the eggs from the lab. But Windler looks embarrassed. "That's not possible," he answers. "I locked the door with my key yesterday. And now I can't find it!"

Daisy, though, always on the job, quickly says, "It's obvious where the missing egg is. Why don't you just return it?"

Why does Daisy suspect that Windler stole the egg?

Stegosaurus

MOONLIGHT VISITOR

Everybody knows that Mr. Linmann's brother Ted, a former astronaut, is visiting him. Everybody also knows that Ted owns a huge collection of moon rocks, and that he plans to exhibit them at the City Center. This is the reason why the Linmanns haven't had a moment's peace since Ted's arrival. Strange people have been lurking around their property. There's even one weird fellow who's been watching their house at night! Nobody knows what he wants. So Mr. Linmann hires Ridley to try to stop this craziness! Ridley is able to photograph the odd stranger one night. But unfortunately, he only gets a shot from the back.

"Let's look in our card file of crooks," Daisy suggests. "This character looks vaguely familiar." Although there are lots and lots of pictures, she soon smiles: "Found him!"

What's his name?

43

Business for Sale

Terry's Barber Shop

This jewel of a shop was founded thirty years ago. Terry's father, Ned, ran the business for more than 25 years, before Terry took it over. 8 chairs and 4 mirrors. Grand location on Hairy Square. Hurry! Call Terry at: (716) 583-9804 First come, first serve.

Thrift Shop

Small shop on Fleaman's Alley. Loaded with stuff. Sale by owner. Own your own business! This is your chance! Call: (712) 765-5698 evenings and Saturdays.

"Chicken Wings" Snack Bar

Best offer !!! Zilly is getting tired. Great opportunity for anybody trying to make a buck! Special prizewinning seasoning. "Best Chicken Wings in Town"! Call Zilly: (719) 559-8703

Kids Playhouse — Day Care Center

New day care center for sale. 50 children, experienced staff. Need to sell because of career change. Write or call: Kids Playhouse 38 Washbear Road 3085 Porktown. Tel. (712) 587-9963

Miscellaneous Ads

Musical Instruments
... instruments second-hand.
Porktown

Looking For Used Books?

10000 titles in stock. fiction, non-fiction, history, military, childrens and juvenile!!! Send two dollars for listi... ...er, 59 ... Str... 3065 Porktown.

Attention:

CLIP CLAP GNAG

PORTIMANT SSEGAME OT LAL BERMEMS FO ETH CLIP CLAP GNAG! TEEMNIG HITS HURTAYDS TA 7:30 PM TA HET ELUB LWO RAB. TOOT ILWL GRINB HET TOOL MORF UOR SLAT GIB GNAB. BEVERYDOY REPNEST ILLW TEG SIH RESHA. BERMEMS OHW NOD'T OWSH, OLSE TOU!!!
OS MOCE!
HET SOBS

Jungle Drops Keep You You...

Three dro... midday and ever... ...s will make... ...! Guaran... Yo... drops w... pla... Dr. Tandl... in the deep... 100, 200 and... shot. Money back... work! Call: (715) 569-4912

Play the Flu...

Classes for beginners, and advanced musicians. Experienced teacher, Rosalie Mellow, will bring

A SUSPICIOUS LITTLE AD

Daisy was called to Gale Scribbler's office. She is the editor-in-chief of the local newspaper. Gale shows Daisy the latest edition of the *Porktown Star*. "Look at this strange ad. It's quite a puzzle to me. I just don't get it," she says. "Unfortunately, none of us noticed it until it was too late. My secretary, Polly, discovered it only when the paper had already been printed," moans Gale miserably.

Daisy looks at the ad, and quickly laughs: "Well, it might not be good for you, but it will help Ridley and me a great deal! These mysterious lines are actually a coded message from the boss of the Clip Clap Gang." Daisy and Ridley have wanted to get hold of this gang for a long time! "Once we decode these words we will know when and where we can trap all of the crooks at the same time," she proudly explains to Gale.

When you decode the ad you'll know what Daisy means.

STRANGE OCCURRENCES AT WHISTLE HORN

The people of Clopperfield are upset. At Castle Whistle Horn, up on the hill, eerie things seem to happen at night. Although nobody lives in the castle anymore, people have often noticed light coming from the tower windows! Some people even claim that they have seen cars driving in and out in the dark of night. Many suspect that a group of crooks have turned the ancient place into their hideout.

It is rumored that there could be counterfeiters up there in the dungeons. "Have Daisy and Ridley check it out," the Major suggests.

And that's how the two detectives end up in front of the big gate of Castle Whistle Horn one evening. The heavy door is shut tightly with four different locks. It appears as if someone else has been trying, unsuccessfully, to get into the castle. Various keys with letter tags lie scattered on the ground. "Four of those keys must fit the locks," Daisy guesses.

Which four keys open the door?

THE FAKE POLICEMAN

Police officer Dave Spottler needs Ridley's help. A short while ago he got a strange phone call. Somebody anonymously threatened to disturb the annual Police Parade, which will take place in the city tomorrow. The creepy caller didn't tell Spottler how he plans to create the disturbance. But he assured him that he will definitely act! "Crooks," Spottler grumbles. "The whole police force will be marching in the parade! Nobody will be available to keep an eye out for that weirdo." So Ridley promises Spottler that he will take care of the matter.

The next day Ridley finds a perfect spot along the parade route, with the best possible view. He's guaranteed to see everything from there! Sure enough, when the police force marches by, Ridley immediately recognizes an imposter in the midst of the many police officers. He must have rented an older uniform, as Ridley spots a slight difference. Now he can pull out the imposter before he is able to disturb the celebration.

Can you also spot the faker?

49

COFFEE AND CAKE FOR FREE

Slip Sordino knows how to get coffee and cake for free! His technique is very simple and, in most cases, successful. He visits cafés and finds a lonely customer to chat with. Once Slip wins the person's trust, he or she enthusiastically invites him for a cup of coffee and a slice of cake.

Winnie Whipple claims to be one of his victims. She fell for Slip's charm in Cliff's Café this afternoon. Luckily, she was able to secretly follow Slip on his way home afterward, so she can tell Daisy the exact address of the con artist. Daisy knows all about Slip's strange habits and has longed to pay him a visit in his shabby attic studio. Now is her chance!

Daisy asks Slip about his acquaintance with Winnie in Cliff's Café. "I don't know anyone by that description, nor have I ever been in that café," he angrily replies. But Daisy doesn't believe Slip. Indeed, she has just noticed something that proves that he is lying!

Do you see what Daisy sees?

AN UNEXPECTED NAP!

Dr. Felix Schnarr is the owner of a well-known arts and sports agency. He is especially proud to represent the world-famous boxer and Tarzan actor, Johnny Walz.

At the moment though, Dr. Schnarr lies sleeping peacefully at his desk. He is holding a pen and next to him is a cup of coffee.

Winnie Scribble, his worried secretary, is shouting at him to wake up! But it's useless. He is fast asleep. Winnie explains to Ridley Long what happened:

"I brought Dr. Schnarr his usual cup of coffee and, shortly after, a letter for him to sign. While signing it he suddenly fell asleep, right in front of me! I immediately ran to Dr. Pillman's office next door. Dr. Pillman and I returned to check on Dr. Schnarr. I realized right away that somebody had stolen Johnny Walz's prized boxing gloves while I was gone. They normally hang on the wall over there! Dr. Pillman found some kind of powder in the coffee that had put Dr. Schnarr to sleep. Someone must have sneaked in here and mixed it with his coffee, before I brought the letter for him to sign. I can't explain it any other way."

"I can," replies Ridley to Winnie. "It was you who put the sleeping powder in Dr. Schnarr's coffee. And while he was asleep you staged the signing of the letter. Because you wanted those boxing gloves so badly!"

How does Ridley Long come to this conclusion?

CHAOS IN
THE PARKING LOT

It's the fifth anniversary of Ridley's and Daisy's detective office—an occasion to celebrate! They decide to throw a big party. The guests flock to the festivities. And they have all parked their cars hurriedly in the building's parking lot, blocking Ridley's and Daisy's car in the back.

The party is in full swing. Everybody is having a great time, until . . . Oh no! It's the telephone ringing! "Not tonight, of all nights," Ridley sighs. But of course crooks aren't invited, so why should they stop working? Much to their dismay, Ridley and Daisy have to leave their own party to crack a new case! Now the chaos in the parking lot is a real problem. Ridley and Daisy have to drive their black car out of there as quickly as possible.

How many cars have to be moved, and in which way, so the two detectives can start on their new case?

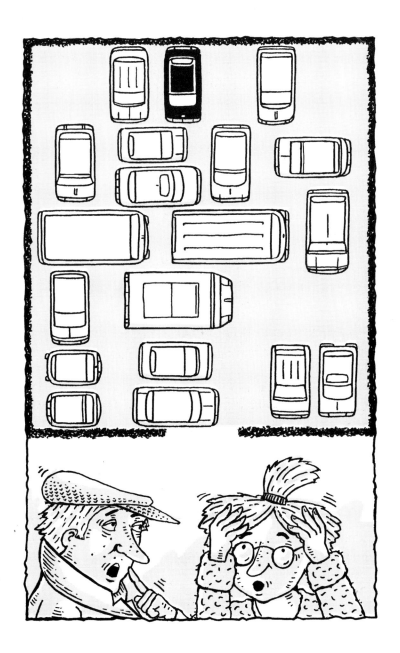

PIZZA AND
OTHER BUSINESS

"Today is Black Thursday," the cashier from the off-track betting office grumbles. He is so upset that Daisy has to calm him down before he can explain what happened. "The scoundrel was betting with a fake ticket," he claims. "And he certainly cashed in a lot of money! I was wondering why the cheater hid his face behind the newspaper. There's one thing I'm sure of: His pants were covered with flour. And after he got the money, he ran toward Joe's Pizza Parlor!"

"I'll check that out," Daisy assures him, and walks over to the pizza parlor.

Joe and his employee, Rudolfo, are behind the counter. Joe is well known in town for his pizza, and surely wouldn't pull such tricks with the horse races. But what about Rudolfo? He could easily have taken a break and just returned from the betting office. Daisy asks Rudolfo where he has spent the last twenty minutes. "Here, of course!" he replies busily. "I just finished three Pizzas Hawaii to go. They are being delivered right this moment."

But Daisy immediately knows that this can't be true. Rudolfo must have been at the betting office.

What makes Daisy so sure?

57

THE MISSING PORKY-SQUIRREL

Swinesville's Botanical Gardens are home to two Porky-Squirrels. They are the only two of their kind left in the country.

Professor Snoop, Peggy, his assistant, and Stew Lens, a photographer, have come a long way in order to study this rare species. They are able to observe them through the wire-mesh fence. One interesting fact is that the squirrels are inseparable. They are always together! But one morning Professor Snoop suddenly spots just one of the squirrels. The second one does not appear all day. "Something is wrong," the scientists agree. But then they begin to suspect each other of having snatched the missing animal. It surely would make an unusual pet! This is a case for Ridley.

They all claim not to have set foot behind the fence. But after a closer look, Ridley comes to a different conclusion. One of them obviously must have been in there and caught the squirrel.

How does Ridley know who stole the squirrel?

SOAPY LAMB CHOPS

When Daisy and her great-aunt were planning a big party to celebrate her eightieth birthday, Daisy recommended the perfect place to hold the party: Kirk's Juicy Bite! The restaurant is run by Kirk Noodle and has a very good reputation. At least it did, until the day of the party.

That's because of the food that Daisy ordered for the feast. It is absolutely disgusting! The guests immediately spit everything out. The lamb chops, the potatoes, even the vegetables taste like soap. Daisy's great-aunt blows a few soap bubbles and then faints.

Kirk Noodle is quite desperate and apologizes profusely. He suspects his brother, Philo, the cook, is behind the embarrassing incident. "My brother threatened me just a short time ago that something bad would happen, because I haven't yet made him my business partner!"

Daisy runs into the kitchen. She wants to know if Philo cooked this miserable meal intentionally. But Philo just shrugs his shoulders. "The meal was fine when I cooked it. Someone else must have done it as a joke." But Daisy quickly sees who the real joker is. None other than Philo!

What does Daisy discover?

THE MYSTERY OF THE "LITTLE MERMAID"

Count Moselstein's chateau is in an uproar this morning. Daisy arrives at 11:30. Duddly Keaton, the butler, nervously leads her into the Count's library. Moselstein is expecting her. He sits, totally devastated, surrounded by piles of books, broken vases, and furniture scattered around the room. The Count arrived just a quarter of an hour ago to find his beloved library in this terrible state.

"Duddly can tell you what happened," he moans. And so the butler begins:

"While the Count was out hunting, two dubious fellows sneaked in here. They ransacked this room looking for something in particular. I arrived while they were tearing down the pictures and the clock from the walls. They quickly grabbed the Count's precious *Little Mermaid* statue from the bureau and ran as fast as they could. The whole thing lasted about five minutes!"

Daisy wants to know more precisely when this happened. Duddly says, "It was 9:15 sharp. That's when I always bring the Count's newspapers into the library."

"Interesting," Daisy says. And after a pause, she adds: "I suggest that you return the *Little Mermaid* instantly. It was you who staged this entire scene, to make it look as if there was a robbery in order to steal the valuable statue yourself!"

Do you know how Daisy comes to this conclusion?

SLUGGER'S SHARP TEETH

Ridley pays his next-door neighbor, Bert Limsky, a visit. They are chatting about bird feed. Just when Bert claims to have found the perfect mixture of grains, his dog, Slugger, dashes through the bushes, barking wildly and running between their legs like a maniac. He is carrying a scrap of fabric in his mouth. "Something weird is going on here," Bert says. He knows his Slugger! They both follow the dog quickly into the garage. Ridley notices at once that someone has been messing with Bert's fancy Oldtimer automobile. All the tires are flat!

"Slugger must have surprised the intruder and stopped him from whatever he was up to," Ridley says.

"Yeah, the crook got away. Too bad," Bert grumbles.

Ridley notes: "But he has left an important piece of proof behind!" And he grabs the shred of fabric in Slugger's snout. "Hurry, we still might be able to catch the no-gooder." They rush outside again to observe the busy street from Bert's garden. "Bingo! There he goes," Ridley laughs.

Can you spot the intruder too?

DESPERATE FOR CHEWING GUM

Yolanda is sitting in her taxi at the crossing of Birch Road and Dunkin Place. She is waiting for her next fare. Over the radio she hears that someone has snatched a whole carton of chewing gum from the Dunkin Candy Store. That special gum with the pictures of famous baseball players! Just then a woman, loaded with shopping bags, jumps into the back of her cab. "To the train station, and hurry!" she shouts.

Yolanda is used to customers being in a rush. But after hearing about the candy-store theft, she grows suspicious. Peeking into the rearview mirror, she notices that the woman in the back is acting rather nervous. Now her suspicions that the chewing-gum thief really is sitting in her taxi mount. "Terrible, what happened at the Dunkin Candy Store," Yolanda mentions nonchalantly.

But the woman dryly replies: "I don't know anything about it. I just shopped on Birch Road."

Now Yolanda is certain that her customer is lying. Via the radio she informs her friend Daisy.

How did the thief give herself away?

IS LOU PAROTTI SINGING IN THE CHORUS?

Ridley dashes around a corner near Waterloo Town Hall. He is following Lou Parotti, the only one of the four Terrible Parotti Brothers who is still on the run. All the others are safely behind bars. Ridley is closing in on the swindler when, strangely, Lou is suddenly gone. He has disappeared!

Ridley comes to a halt in front of Town Hall to catch his breath. "Where did the crook go?" he wonders. Just then he hears a chorus singing through the half-open door. "That's it!" Ridley shouts. "Lou must have slipped into Town Hall to hide." Ridley enters the building and finds himself in the midst of the rehearsal of the Waterloo Chorus. No trace of Lou! "But hold on a minute," Ridley reasons. "Perhaps Lou has become a member of the chorus."

Is Ridley's suspicion correct?

69

For Milly:
Start at T.S. - go straight, first right, third left, next left, next left, second right, third right, next left, next left, second right, next left, next right, second left. - You are there. Ring doorbell three times!
Nose Gang

LEFT OR RIGHT . . .

Daisy is inconsolable. She was just about to nab Bad Milly. Bad Milly is a member of the Nose Gang, a group involved in shady business of all kinds. Daisy noticed Bad Milly just a moment ago in the Train Station Coffee Shop. But it appears that Milly recognized Daisy, too, and slipped away. In her rush, though, Bad Milly dropped a piece of paper on the floor. At first Daisy is puzzled by the weird jottings on the note. But after careful consideration, she has an idea what the scribbling is all about. She reaches for her map of the town and soon everything fits into place. Bad Milly must be on her way to deliver top-secret information to her gang. But even Bad Milly doesn't know where the other crooks are. It looks as if the note is a guide to their current hideout.

"Great, this means that perhaps I can catch the whole Nose Gang at once," Daisy thinks, and she is ready to go. According to the paper the chase begins right at the train station.

Where will Daisy meet the Nose Gang?

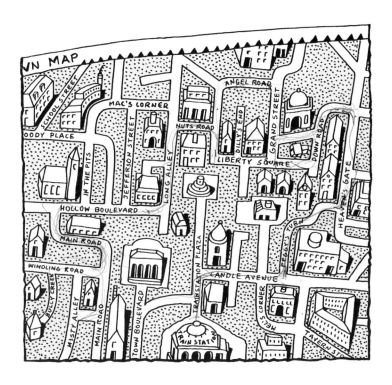

THE LITTLE RED THUNDERBIRD

 When Ridley picks up the phone, he hears many different voices and clinking glasses in the background. Then Vincent Toyle, an antiques dealer, shouts: "Please come over quickly. My little red Thunderbird has just been stolen!"

As soon as Ridley arrives at Toyle's store he learns that the little red Thunderbird happens to be a valuable antique toy car.

Toyle explains what happened: "I was on the first floor of my store. I didn't know there was a customer upstairs on the second floor. All of a sudden I saw a man running down the stairs. I could see that he was hiding something under his coat. The chap dashed out the door. When I rushed after him he disappeared into the bar across the street. Unfortunately I lost sight of him in the crowd. The rest you already know. I called you from there."

Ridley goes over to the bar and takes a look. Then he follows Toyle upstairs to the second floor of his store. He examines the case where the little red Thunderbird had been displayed. "Is this valuable toy car insured against theft?" Ridley wants to know.

"Yes," Toyle answers. "Luckily I insured it just last week."

Ridley smiles. "That's what I thought! Your story doesn't wash with me, and the insurance company won't believe it either."

How does Ridley know that Toyle is lying and trying to cheat the insurance company?

THE CLUE IN THE PICTURE PUZZLE

Daisy empties the anonymous envelope onto her desk, and sighs: "Darn, another one of these encoded messages!" Her desk is covered with pictures. Thankfully, there is also a note, which says: "When you solve this riddle you will be able to catch a big fish. The boss of the spy ring Secret Dogs! He will be disguised as an artist and perform in Jolly's Variety Show.—A Friend"

Looking carefully, Daisy quickly realizes that the small pictures contain letters and show enlarged details of the bigger pictures with numbers. The numbers imply

the correct order of the letters. When they are put together, they reveal which performer the boss of the Secret Dogs will be disguised as.

Can you figure it out?

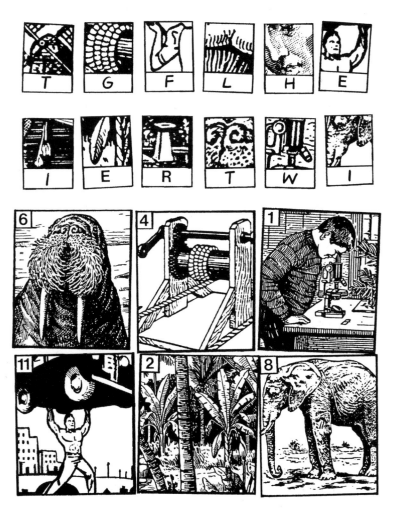

SPIRO, THE GRAND INVENTOR

Every Friday Ridley meets his friends at Stamper's, the stamp collectors' café. But before joining them he usually visits his friend Spiro Finder. Spiro is an eccentric inventor of strange engines and exotic appliances. He lives right across from Stamper's.

But today Ridley finds Spiro in total despair. No wonder, his newest invention is completely wrecked! Spiro moans: "I was out of the house yesterday afternoon. When I returned I found this mess. Someone has intentionally destroyed my automatic teeth-cleaning engine for dogs! I have a hunch it was Stiffman, my landlord. I haven't been able to pay my rent for the last couple of months. He warned me that something would happen soon if I don't pay."

Just then, they see Stiffman walking by. Ridley asks him directly if he had been in Spiro's place yesterday, and if he had anything to do with the wrecked invention. But Stiffman angrily answers: "Not a chance! I couldn't have been there. I was at Stamper's from two o'clock in the afternoon until eleven o'clock at night. Some friends and I were playing cards."

Ridley smiles. "Impossible! And one lie leads to another! You must have been here, destroying Spiro's new invention!"

How does Ridley know that Stiffman is lying?

SHORTY ON THE RUN

Shorty has done it again! With one of his many tricks he has made Don Chapplow's wallet a little lighter. But Chapplow informed Daisy immediately, and she is about to catch up with Shorty. Not quite, though–because he still has a small lead. Daisy follows him to the highway. There she loses track of him. She stands at a nearby construction site. Just then she notices the workers leaving the shed after their lunch break. But a peek through the window tells her that someone else must have had his picnic in there too, just after the others left. Is it Shorty? Daisy enters the place and takes a look. But she can't find anybody in the room. Has Shorty seen her and fled through the open window?

Or is he still in the shed?

THE MANY FACES OF DR. KIMBERLY

Dr. Kimberly is one of the most feared gamblers in town. He knows his business! With his crooked tricks he has already emptied several casino banks. And he hasn't ever been caught. It's because he has so many different faces. He is a master of disguise! Sometimes he appears as a young cool fellow. Sometimes he turns up as an old man or even as a lady! It's not unusual for him to change his appearance a number of times in one evening. Just yesterday Dr. Kimberly successfully cheated again at the Domino Casino. It was only later that they realized that most of the evening's winners were in fact one and the

same person: Dr. Kimberly! The casino recently installed secret cameras that film all the casino's guests. Luckily, Kimberly was caught on camera doing his dirty work. So Bob Casher, the director of the Domino Casino, shows Ridley twelve portrait photographs. They were all taken at the roulette table yesterday evening. Ridley decides to find out which characters are actually Dr. Kimberly, so he can warn other casinos of the cheater.

How many times can you spot Dr. Kimberly in the twelve pictures?

A LOVE LETTER IN THE WRONG HANDS

Daisy loves to go to the circus. Today she treats herself to the Bubble Brothers' Circus. She can't wait to see the famous dwarf-pig balancing act. However, the atmosphere in the ring is tense. Esmillia, the trapeze artist, is broken-hearted. Clown Valentino's wonderful love letter to her has disappeared overnight. She had put it in the night table next to her bed. This morning it was gone! Someone must have sneaked into her camper and taken it. Esmillia slept very deeply last night and didn't hear a thing.

After the show Daisy decides to see whether she can help Esmillia. She visits her in her camper. But Esmillia is not alone. Luzia, the dancer, sits next to her on the bed and tries to comfort her. "Isn't it terrible," Luzia says. "I came right over after I heard what happened!"

Daisy looks around in Esmillia's cozy camper. Then she smiles: "Lots of thieves come back to the scene of the crime. It seems you do too, Luzia. I think you are in love with Valentino as well. That's not a good reason, though, to steal his letter to Esmillia. Give it back to her at once!"

Why does Daisy suspect Luzia stole the letter?

THE PARROT AND A BROKEN WINDOW

Mrs. Birdsley shows Daisy the broken window, and explains: "Last night I heard someone sneaking down the stairs in the hallway. It was just about midnight. Shortly afterward, a stone, thrown from the backyard, flew through the glass of my window. A piece of paper was wrapped around the stone and on it was written: "If you don't put a stop to your parrot's endless squawking, I will! And it will never make another sound again!'"

Mr. Chappel:
"Yesterday evening I didn't feel well, so I went to bed at 8 o'clock. I slept very deeply and didn't hear a thing. I only noticed Mrs. Birdsley's parrot squawking once!"

Mr. and Mrs. Bullow:
"We watched TV last night. At 11 o'clock we went to bed. We're not the kind of people who throw stones into other neighbors' windows!"

Daisy immediately pays Mrs. Birdsley's neighbors a visit. She asks them all the same question: "Last night someone threw a stone through Mrs. Birdsley's window. Where were you at that time?"

After they answer, Daisy knows who threw the threatening stone.

Who do you think it was?

Here are their answers:

Mrs. Monroe:
"Last night I visited a friend until 9:45. When I got home I went straight to bed. So by midnight I had already been sleeping for two hours."

The Calmly twins:
"Yesterday evening we were at a friend's birthday party. We were back home by 11:15. We didn't notice anybody throwing stones."

THE TEMPTING REWARD

Ridley and Rudy Billington, a bank director, stand help-lessly in front of the Town Bank. Just minutes ago the bank had been "visited" by a couple of shady characters no bank likes! They stole a box with golden paper clips, an annual gift for the bank's loyal customers. Ridley and Billington debate what should be done next. Unfortunately the robbers got away, leaving no trace behind them.

Billington is furious. He angrily shouts: "I offer a reward to anyone giving information that helps to catch these robbers!"

Diana Schmalz, across the street, has heard the tempt-ing announcement. Immediately she rushes over. "I saw it happen," she claims. "I had just stepped out of the gro-cery store across the street. That's when I saw some men running out of the bank. They jumped into a green van and drove off toward Lemon Avenue."

Rudy Billington is obviously relieved to hear Diana's information. "At least we now know that the crooks drive a green van." Ridley, however, looks skeptical.

"You are just out for the reward," he asserts. "Your story can't be true."

How does Ridley know that Diana Schmalz's story is invented?

ANSWERS

Page 8
The Mysterious Moustache
Daisy notices wet shoes and an umbrella on the floor in
Schlotzing's bathroom. They prove that Nero must have been
outside in the rain just a short time ago. So he obviously is
lying.

Page 11
The Narrow Escape
The man on the stairs with the suitcase (to the left of the waving
boy with the backpack) is the smuggler. He noticed Ridley and
took off before Ridley could act.

Page 12
Wanted
Dino is just leaving the dressing room on the far left of
the picture.

Page 14
Is Hobbard Mansion Stalky's Hideout?
Daisy has discovered a candle in the lower right window.
Compare the candle in the left-hand picture to the same candle
in the morning, on the right page, where it's only about half the
size. Therefore, it must have been lit during the night.

Page 17
The Top-Secret Mars Vehicle
Will Poke claims to have forgotten his glasses at home and thus wouldn't be able to read the secret documents. But he seems to be able to read the newspaper on his desk without them. He must be lying.

Page 18
The Odd Safe
Punch the digits 5, 3, 3, 8, into your calculator and then look at the number upside down. You will read the word BEES. That's what Ridley discovers. So the four-digit number is 5, 3, 3, 8.

Page 20
Who Is Zoro in Real Life?
The seven-digit number is 443-7923. That's Zoro's telephone number. His real name is Floyd Murkey, and he lives at 3 Ellwood Road.

Page 22
Cigars in Deep Snow
Kirk Mouser is the cigar thief and must be lying. One can see the prints of his shoes and cane coming around the corner. They clearly show that Kirk didn't just walk by Cole's shop but that he also went inside.

Page 24
Swinesgate Porcelain
If Trickler had fled through the abandoned tunnel, the spider-web across the opening would have been torn and the plants would have been trampled.

Page 26
A Game with Shirt Buttons
Trenton claims that he hadn't been in Nick's tavern. But since he is wearing only an undershirt—and his jacket is hanging on a chair in the tavern—this can't be true. He clearly must have been in there a while ago and played the slot machine.

Page 28
The Man Who Loves Beds
On the videotape Max wears striped socks and on the night table are his sneakers. The person carryng the mattress in the left-hand corner (you can just see his feet under the mattress) wears the same socks and sneakers. Daisy's suspicion is correct: Max leaves Sleepyland disguised as a deliveryman.

Page 31
The Fake Pacissto
The two identical paintings are in the middle of the top row and in the second row from the bottom on the left.

Page 32
Phony Magic
Abra Kabra is in the back room of the bar. The smoke rings in the air are the same as the ones on the poster at the entrance to Abra Kabra's magic show.

Page 34
The Precious Louis Philippe
If you read carefully you will know that the little Louis Philippe is usually ten minutes slow. According to the poster in Waddler's store all his clocks run on time. They all show 11:45 except the Louis Philippe, which shows 11:35 on its face. It is on the lowest shelf of the showcase.

Page 36
Transaction at the Snack Bar
The two spies have exchanged newspapers. The secret information is on a disc in Will's *New Post*.

Page 38
Heck Dundee and the Cello
If Heck doesn't know about the cello, as he claims, why didn't he also trip over it in the dark? Instead, he automatically walked around it while going to get the light from the kitchen. He must have known about it because he put it there himself.

Page 40
The Missing Dinosaur Egg
Assistant Windler must have stolen the third egg. Too bad he lost his key to the lab in the Dino Park when he climbed over the glass fence. The key with the tag is lying in the grass at the right side of the picture, next to Daisy.

Page 42
Moonlight Visitor
The stranger's name is Klimo Katz. You can recognize him by his big glasses, his large ears sticking out, and the cap he is holding in the photograph. He did want to snatch one of Ted's valuable moon rocks.

Page 45
A Suspicious Little Ad
The ad is an encoded message to all members of the Clip Clap Gang. The letters of each word are scrambled.
Attention:
Clip Clap Gang
IMPORTANT MESSAGE TO ALL MEMBERS OF THE CLIP CLAP GANG! MEETING THIS THURSDAY AT 7:30 PM AT THE BLUE OWL BAR. OTTO WILL BRING THE LOOT FROM OUR LAST BIG BANG. EVERYBODY PRESENT WILL GET HIS SHARE. MEMBERS WHO DON'T SHOW, LOSE OUT!!!
SO COME!
THE BOSS

Page 46
Strange Occurrences at Whistle Horn
Key I opens lock 1. Key Q opens lock 2. Key L opens lock 3. Key B opens lock 4.

Page 48
The Fake Policeman
The fake policeman is in the sixth row from the front. He is the second policeman from the left in the row.

Page 50
Coffee and Cake for Free
Slip Sordino knows Cliff's Café very well! He must have been
there because there is a package of matches with the café's logo
lying on the round table. It's in the lower right corner of the picture.

Page 53
An Unexpected Nap!
Winnie Scribble did put the sleeping powder in Dr. Schnarr's
coffee. And when he fell asleep, she placed the letter in front of
him, put the pen in his hand and walked off with the boxing
gloves. But putting the pen into Dr. Schnarr's right hand was a
big mistake. The photographs on the bookcase clearly show that
Dr. Schnarr is left-handed.

Page 54
Chaos in the Parking Lot
Fifteen cars have to be moved before Ridley and Daisy can
finally drive off.

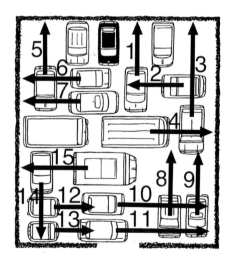

Page 56
Pizza and Other Business
Daisy has spotted the poster in the upper left-hand corner of the picture. It says that Pizza Hawaii is available only on Saturdays and Sundays. But today is "Black Thursday." So Rudolfo couldn't have prepared any Pizzas Hawaii. He was at the off-track betting office using the fake ticket.

Page 58
The Missing Porky-Squirrel
Stew Lens must have been in the Botanical Gardens to snatch the Porky-Squirrel. He accidentally dropped a roll of film under a bush on the left, just above Ridley's head. Of course Ridley discovered this at once!

Page 61
Soapy Lamb Chops
Philo is definitely lying. Why would he have a bottle of liquid soap among all the cooking ingredients? The soap is behind the blender, to its right. Bon appetit! .

Page 62
The Mystery of the "Little Mermaid"
Duddly, the butler, claims that he surprised the robbers at 9:15 in the library, just when they tore down the pictures and the clock from the walls. This would have made the clock stop ticking right then. Yet the clock face shows exactly 10 o'clock. This proves that the clock was thrown to the floor at 10 o'clock. Duddly staged the robbery himself to steal the *Little Mermaid*.

Page 64
Slugger's Sharp Teeth
The intruder is walking off with his bicycle on the left side of the picture. A piece of fabric from his pants is missing.

Page 67
Desperate for Chewing Gum
Yolanda notices in the mirror the logo of the Dunkin Candy Store on one of her customer's shopping bags. So the lady has not only been on Dunkin Place, but even in the candy store. Since she denies that fact, she most likely has stolen the chewing gum.

Page 68
Is Lou Parotti Singing in the Chorus?
Ridley's suspicion is correct. Lou has sneaked into the chorus. But he must be singing badly, since he is holding the sheet music upside down. He is second from the right in the second row from the bottom.

Page 70
Left or Right . . .
If Daisy follows the directions she will meet Bad Milly, and probably the whole Nose Gang, in a little house on Bully Creek.

Page 72
The Little Red Thunderbird
Toyle claims that he saw the thief running down the stairs hiding something under his coat. How does he know that it is the little red Thunderbird? He says he followed the man into the bar across the street. So he didn't check upstairs to see what was missing first. He called Ridley right from the bar. He clearly has invented his story to cheat the insurance company!

Page 74
The Clue in the Picture Puzzle
Tonight, in Jolly's Variety Show, the boss of the Secret Dogs will perform disguised as a weight lifter. Good luck, Daisy!

Page 77
Spiro, the Grand Inventor
Stiffman couldn't have been in Stamper's Café on Thursday afternoon and evening. On the sign in the window of Stamper's Café, across the street from Spiro's, it states that the café is closed on Thursdays.

Page 79
Shorty on the Run
There are no clues that Shorty fled through the window or the skylight. So take a good look at the clothing in the back. Shorty has hidden himself behind the coats. You can spot his pants and shoes.

Page 80
The Many Faces of Dr. Kimberly
Dr. Kimberly can't change his nose, eyes, and ears. With these attributes you will recognize him six times in the picture collection: B, D, F, G, I, L.

Page 82
A Love Letter in the Wrong Hands
Daisy noticed that Luzia is wearing only one earring. The second one of the pair is lying on the floor under Esmillia's bed. Luzia must have lost it at night when she sneaked into Esmillia's camper to steal Valentino's love letter. Luzia noticed the loss this morning. She came back to Esmillia's to look for the earring, so it wouldn't give her away.

Page 84
The Parrot and a Broken Window
Mrs. Monroe must have thrown the stone. How else would she know that it happened exactly at midnight? Daisy referred only to "last night" when she questioned the neighbors.

Page 86
The Tempting Reward
Diana claims that she saw the men running out of the bank and jumping into a green van just when she stepped out of the grocery store. This can't be true, since the delivery truck from Frostlake was parked in front of the store, blocking her view. All she would have been able to see was that truck!

ABOUT THE AUTHOR/ ARTIST

Jürg Obrist studied photography at the Arts and Crafts School in Zurich, Switzerland. He then moved to the United States, where he lived for many years. At the moment he is back in Zurich with his family, doing freelance illustration and writing articles for teen magazines.

The author originally wrote this book in German, but his years in the United States perfected his English to the point that he was also able to be the translator for this edition. The job was a particular challenge because the words in the artwork had to be translated–but no problem. Jürg is also the illustrator of the original edition, so he was able to redo the calligraphy as well.

This is the second in a series of three mini-mystery books, all of which have been very popular with young would-be detectives in Germany as well as in France and South Korea. The first book in the series is *Case Closed?! Forty Mini-Mysteries for You to Solve.*